Jackula the Vampire Dog

by Ian Punnett

illustrated by D.C. Ice

Lydia -
Happy Halloween -
Thanks for coming
to the Art Crawl!

Of all the sad things that are,
losing a dog to a car
is a feeling I hope
you don't feel.

A mean cat two doors down
chased my puppy uptown
where she was hit by a
speeding car's wheel.

Because of that fright,
I couldn't sleep nights.
There are things that
you just can't un-see.

When one night it was raining,
I was on my knees praying,
and this is what happened
to me.

As I asked for God's help,
I heard a dog's yelp.
I went to our door in the back.

Against the night's storm
was a soaking-wet form.
His dog tag was smudged
but for "Jack."

I invited Jack in.
Who knows where he'd been?
I took him upstairs to my bed.

On my covers he crept,
but I don't think he slept.
Poor Jack looked almost
half dead.

It was the first night that I'd
slept well and not cried.
Jack was guarding me
whenever I peeked.

So early the next day,
Mom said, "This dog can stay,
but only a few days—
or a week."

That's just how it went.
Every daytime was spent
with Jack sleeping till
after twilight.

And then he hovered over me
as my quilt covered over me,
I was never once out of
his sight.

My mother who loves me,
who always thinks of me,
said, "Do you want Jack
to be your new pet?

"Then follow my rule
and today after school
have him checked by
Dr. Helsing, our vet."

On the walk there Jack stayed
so carefully in the shade.
We waited till Dr. Helsing
was free.

The minute he saw Jack
he was taken aback.
"All about this new dog,
please tell me!"

He then listened with wonder
how Jack arrived with
the thunder
and then told me something
much scarier.

"Your new dog is not
what you think you just got.
Jack is a Transylvanian terrier!"

"Transylvanian!" I gasped.
"Is that a problem?" I asked.
"Depends," he said, "on what
Jack's been eating."

I said, "Now that you
mention it,
I never had questioned it,
but Jack really hasn't
been feeding!"

He said, "If I don't misjudge,
when I clean off this smudge,
it will reveal your dog's
secret ID!"

Using spit and a rag,
he cleaned off Jack's tag:
Jackula the Vampire Dog—
OMG!

"My mother will freak!
Of this do not speak!
Doctor, do you know of
a cure?"

"Your mom will be fine.
We will tell her in time.
But there's one thing
of which I am sure.

"While I try to treat him,
you'll have to feed him
the food of his
vampire-dog world.

"In you I confide,
he must go outside
and drink the blood of a
neighborhood squirrel!"

What should I do with that?
Could Jack go through
with that?
So while my mother was
sleeping downstairs . . .

As the night breeze
was blowing,
with more trusting than knowing,
I watched Jackula float
out in the air.

First he did some backflips
and some other Jack-tricks—
my grin couldn't have been
any grinner.

Jack waved "bye" in a hurry
when he saw a squirrel scurry,
and he flew off to get some
fresh dinner!

The next morning at dawn
I looked out on our lawn,
and I had a couple of shocks!

Believe it or not he
left a bushy squirrel body
drained like an empty
juice box!

And it would not be his last!
They started piling up fast,
these victims of my
bloodsucking friend.

Before dawn could crackula,
there would be Jackula
watching from the bed's
other end.

And that's just where
we'll leave it.
I hope you believe it!
No word yet from Dr. Helsing.

My new dog and me,
nervous squirrels in my tree,
and—oh, there is
one more thing!

I hate to end my story
on something so gory
but remember that cat
living near?

I'm not saying Jack did it—
and I'm not saying he didn't—
but I haven't seen that cat
in a year!

Shhhh . . .

ISBN: 978-1-59298-425-1

Library of Congress Control Number: 2011931704
Printed in the United States of America
First Printing: 2011

15   14   13   12   11   6   5   4   3   2   1

 BEAVER'S POND
PRESS

Beaver's Pond Press, Inc.
7104 Ohms Lane, Suite 101
Edina, MN 55439-2129
(952) 829-8818
www.BeaversPondPress.com

To order, visit www.BeaversPondBooks.com
or call (800) 901-3480. Reseller discounts available.

Project management by Margery Punnett, Urban Cottage Company
Book design by Mayfly Design (mayflydesign.net)